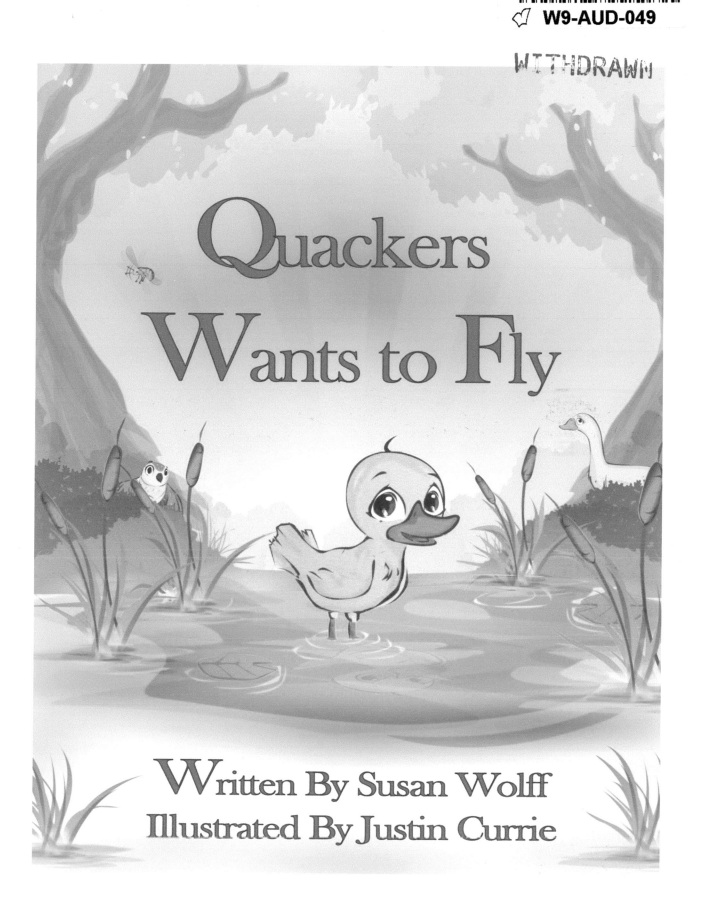

Quackers Wants to Fly

Written By Susan Wolff
Illustrated By Justin Currie

Quackers Wants to Fly

SkyHigh Tales

A Division of High Hill Press

SkyHigh Tales, a division of High Hill Press, USA

Written by Susan Wolff
Illustrated by Justin Currie

Quackers Wants to Fly, 2013, first in the Friends at the Pond Series, by Susan Wolff

ISBN: 978-1-60653-074-0
Library of Congress Catalog Number in Publication Data.
First **SkyHigh Tales** Edition: 2013

0123456789

www.highhillpress.com
www.friendsatthepond.com

Dedicated to my special "Ducklings."

This book belongs to:

Deerfield Public Library.
Dream Big.
Susan Wolff

Quackers the Duck lives here.

Next to a pond, in a patch of grass.

Quackers can do lots of things.

Quackers can waddle.

Quackers can swim.

Quackers can flap his wings. Quackers can
Quack. "Quack, quack."

But there is one thing
Quackers can't do. Quackers can't fly.

"Come fly with us," call the ducks at the pond.

Quackers tries. He waddles. He quacks. He flaps. But he can't fly.
"That's my problem," Quackers cries. "I can't fly."

Mommy and Daddy Duck smile. "You are our
special duckling. We love how you
waddle. We watch you swim.
We listen for your quack.
One day, you will fly."

Quackers doesn't want to wait. "I know!" exclaims Quackers. "I will ask my friends at the pond for help." So, off Quackers waddles to find Ollie the Wise Owl.

"Ollie, wake up! I have a problem. I can't fly."

"You can't fly?" asks Ollie. "When I was an owlet, I couldn't fly."

"I waited until my fluffy feathers changed to flying feathers. One night, I raised my wings and I was flying around the moonbeams. 1,2,3,4,5! Count the falling, fluffy feathers," Ollie hoots.

"I like to count," Quackers tells his friend.

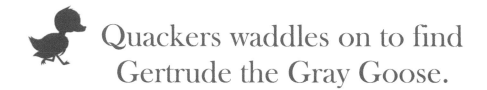 Quackers waddles on to find
Gertrude the Gray Goose.

"Honk, honk, how are you?" asks Gertrude.

"Gertrude, I have a problem. I can't fly."

"You can't fly? Tsk, tsk," says Gertrude. "When
I was a gosling, I couldn't fly. My granny told
me to wait for the bees to make honey."

"I watched the bees and with a buzz and a hum, 1,2,3,4,5, honey began to drip from the bee hive. Wait for the honey," says Gertrude.

"Mmm, I love honey," smacks Quackers.

All of a sudden, there is a twirling,
a whirling,
a whoosh!!!
It's Dena the Dragonfly.

"Quackers, why aren't you flying with
the other ducks?" asks Dena.

"That's my problem,"
mumbles Quackers. "I can't fly."

"You can't fly?" whirs Dena. "When I was a nymph, I couldn't fly. I was tiny. Slowly, my body grew and my eyes got bigger. One day, poof! I turned into a dragonfly and fluttered away. Watch the nymphs at the pond. See you later, Quackers."

Quackers thanks his friends at the pond. "I have a lot to think about."

Just then, uh, oh! Quackers hears a noise.
A duckling is sitting by the pond. She is crying.

"Why are you so sad?" asks Quackers.

"My name is Clementine and I have a
problem.
I can swim. I can quack
and flap my wings.
But I can't fly."

"Oh, my!" says Quackers. "I have the same problem."
Quackers tells Clementine about the owlet's fluffy feathers. He tells her about the bees making honey and the nymphs changing at the pond. Clementine likes Quackers. Quackers likes Clementine.

They waddle and flap.

They quack.

They play.

Suddenly, pop! Quackers has an idea.

Together, Clementine and Quackers count owlet's fluffy feathers. 1,2,3,4,5.

Quackers and Clementine peek at the busy bees.
They wait. Soon honey is dripping from the hive.

"Yum, yum."

"Follow me, Clementine," says Quackers.

Side by side, they watch the nymphs change. Whoosh! Whoosh! Beautiful dragonflies fly from the pond.

One day, at the pond, the ducks call to Quackers and Clementine. "Come fly with us."

Quackers tries.
He waddles.
He quacks.
He flaps.

Clementine tries. She waddles. She quacks. She flaps.

At that very moment, Quackers and Clementine
spread their wings.

Up, up, they go.

Mommy and Daddy Duck smile.
They are proud.

"Wow," cheer their friends at the pond.

"Quack, quack," shouts Quackers. "Look at me.
I waited. I grew. I changed. Finally, I can fly.
Clementine too."
"Oh, MY!"

The End

Susan Wolff is a retired elementary school teacher living in the Chicago area. Sue loved reading to her students and continues to read to her grandchildren. She hopes that *Quackers Wants to Fly* inspires young readers to spread their wings and try new things.

Justin Currie grew up on a small farm outside the village of La Riviere, Canada. He is a full time video concept artist and in his spare time he enjoys illustrating children's books. He also attends international Comic Conventions where he sells his artwork.

Watch for more stories from Susan Wolff's Friends at the Pond book series.